LUBNA and PEBBLE

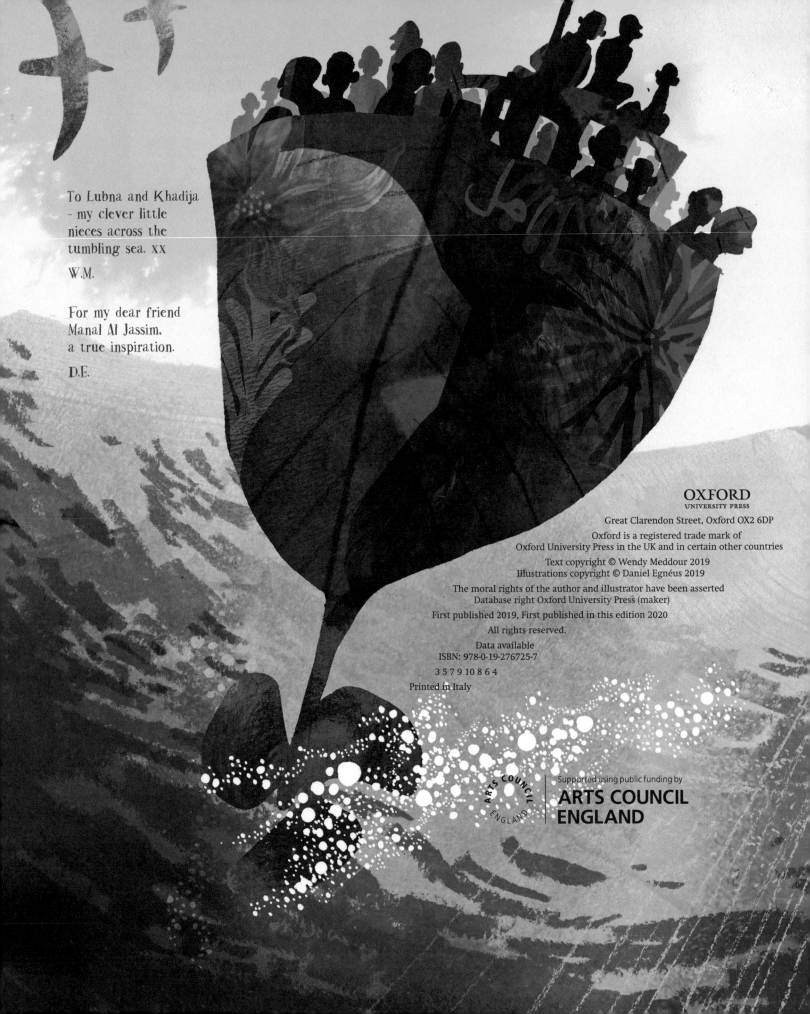

To Lubna and Khadija
- my clever little
nieces across the
tumbling sea. xx

W.M.

For my dear friend
Manal Al Jassim,
a true inspiration.

D.E.

OXFORD
UNIVERSITY PRESS

Great Clarendon Street, Oxford OX2 6DP

Oxford is a registered trade mark of
Oxford University Press in the UK and in certain other countries

Text copyright © Wendy Meddour 2019
Illustrations copyright © Daniel Egnéus 2019

The moral rights of the author and illustrator have been asserted
Database right Oxford University Press (maker)

First published 2019, First published in this edition 2020

Data available
ISBN: 978-0-19-276725-7

3 5 7 9 10 8 6 4

Printed in Italy

ARTS COUNCIL
ENGLAND

Supported using public funding by
ARTS COUNCIL
ENGLAND

LUBNA
and PEBBLE

WENDY MEDDOUR

DANIEL EGNÉUS

OXFORD

UNIVERSITY PRESS

Lubna's best friend was a pebble.
It was shiny and smooth and grey.

Lubna found it on the beach when they arrived in the night.

Then she fell asleep in Daddy's salty arms.

When Lubna opened her
eyes, it was morning.

They had landed in
a World of Tents.

Lubna clutched Daddy's
hand and gripped
her pebble.

Somehow, she knew they'd keep her safe.

In a big white tent,
Lubna found a felt-tip pen.

She drew a happy
face on her pebble.

'Hello, Pebble,'
whispered Lubna.

Pebble smiled back.

Lubna told Pebble everything.
About her brothers.
About home.
About the war.

Pebble always listened to her stories.
Pebble always smiled when she felt scared.

'I love you, Pebble,' sighed Lubna.

Then, the winter arrived. The winds began to blow. The tents began to flap.

Daddy said, 'Come close,
I'll keep you warm.'

But Lubna was worried.
'What if Pebble gets a cold?'

'That must *never* happen,' said Daddy.
He went and found a shoebox and a tea towel.

'Thank you,' Lubna grinned.

Then she put Pebble to bed and kissed it goodnight.

Soon, a little
boy arrived.

At first, he had no words.
Just blinks and sneezes
and stares.

'This is my best friend, Pebble,'
Lubna said.

The little boy coughed.
And sneezed.
Then smiled.

'Hello, Pebble.
My name's Amir.'

Lubna and Amir became friends.
They played 'Hide and Seek'
underneath the stars.

But at bedtime, Lubna
whispered to Pebble,
'You are *still* my
best friend.'

One day,
Daddy was beaming.

'We are leaving.
We have found
a new home!'

Lubna felt happy.
Then sad.

Amir cried.

That night, Lubna couldn't sleep.
She asked Pebble what to do.

Pebble didn't answer.

But by the morning,
Lubna knew.

Lubna gave Amir the
shoebox and the pen.

'What do I do if
Pebble misses you?'
asked Amir.

'Draw the smile
back on,' said Lubna.

'And what do I do if
I miss you?'

'Tell Pebble all about it,' Lubna said.
Amir nodded and held the shoebox tight.

'Goodbye, Pebble,'
Lubna whispered.

'Hello, Pebble,'
Amir said.